Springboard Series

Danger on Broken Arrow Trail

by Alex B. Allen

Pictures by Michael Norman

ALBERT WHITMAN & Company, Chicago

Other Books in the Springboard Series

BASKETBALL TOSS-UP
FIFTH DOWN
NO PLACE FOR BASEBALL
ROD-AND-REEL TROUBLE

Library of Congress Cataloging in Publication Data
Allen, Alex B.
    Danger on Broken Arrow Trail.

    (Springboard series)
    SUMMARY: Beth and her friend Sally combine
ingenuity, hiking know-how, and common sense to track
down Kevin when they become separated hiking in the
woods.
    [1. Hiking—Fiction] I. Norman, Michael, ill.
II. Title.
PZ7.A4217Dan   [Fic]   74-19499
ISBN 0-8075-1455-1

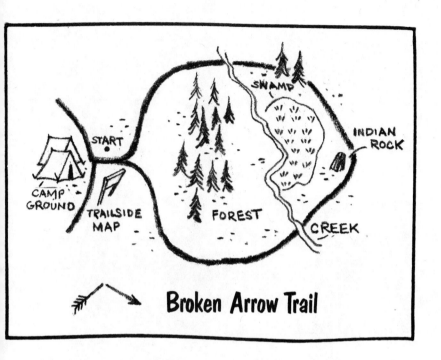

Broken Arrow Trail

Contents:

❖│❖

Camp in the Woods

"Hold that pole up!" Mr. Star shouted to Kevin.

"I can't reach high enough, Dad!"

The tent pole came apart in the middle. The canvas settled slowly over Kevin and Mr. Star.

"Help!" shouted Kevin. "Get us out!"

"Will you look at that?" laughed Mrs. Star. "Our two big rugged campers!"

Beth and her friend Sally looked over at the funny shaped tent with two moving humps underneath it.

"Help!" shouted Kevin again.

Beth and Sally ran over and felt around for the opening of the tent. When they found it, they pulled it open and held it up. Kevin

5

scrambled out on his hands and knees. His father lifted the canvas and walked out.

"Well, Kevin," smiled Mr. Star, "maybe next year you'll be tall enough to reach that top pole."

"I wish it could be next year now," said Kevin. "I'd like to be tall as a totem pole."

"Totem pole!" laughed Beth. "Is that all you ever think about—Indians?"

"I've decided on a new name for myself," said Kevin. "From now on I'm Soaring Eagle."

Mrs. Star laughed. "And last week it was Running Horse. What will it be next week?"

Everyone pitched in. Soon the two tents were up and their home in the woods ready for them. The campers looked around.

The Stars had been planning this trip for a long time. They tried to go camping every year. Last year Mr. and Mrs. Star had gone alone. They had found this quiet campground deep in the north woods.

"Aren't we lucky Mom and Dad wanted to show us this special place?" Beth said happily to Sally. "And here we are, all set to explore."

"It's beautiful," said Sally. "I've never seen so many Christmas trees in one place." She had come along with the Stars because she was Beth's best friend. Each year Kevin or Beth brought a friend, and this year it was Beth's turn.

"It looks scary out there, though," Sally went on. "Beautiful, but scary. I've never been anywhere like this before." She pointed to the woods that closed in the campground.

"It's not scary!" said Kevin. "It's exciting."

"You're right, Soaring Eagle," said Beth. "Really, Sally, you'll love it. There's so much to see and do in the woods."

"You'll see, Sally," said Kevin.

"No, I won't," said Sally. "I'll stay right here in the open where it's safe and sound." She pulled a book from her sweater pocket. "I'll finish my book while you explore."

"Nothing doing," answered Beth. "Dad says there's a great trail here. We'll all try it."

Kevin chimed in. "Broken Arrow Trail. Let's hike it now! It loops right back on itself. You can always get back to the beginning.

There's no way to get lost on a trail like that."

"A hike in those woods?" asked Sally. "With maybe wolves and bears and wild animals like that? No thanks."

Mr. Star heard Sally. "No chance of seeing any wolves, Sally. They've all moved north, out of the state. We may still have a bear or two around here, but they stay as far away from people as they can. It's safe or we wouldn't let Sally and Kevin explore on their own."

"But you know I've never been in the woods before," Sally said. "I didn't think it would be, well, so big. What if we get lost?"

"Oh, don't worry about that," Mrs. Star smiled and said. "If you stay on the trail you can't possibly get lost. We hiked it last year and it's a good trail. Besides, you have Soaring Eagle, our Indian guide, to show you around."

"Are you coming, too?" Sally looked at Mr. and Mrs. Star, hoping they would come along.

"Nope," said Mr. Star. "I'm getting our fishing tackle together right now. Mrs. Star and I are going out to catch your dinner."

"Come on," Kevin shouted at the girls. "Let's get moving!"

Sally couldn't help laughing. "Okay, I'll go. But I need an Indian name, too. How about Princess Trembling Leaf?"

"Hey," called Mrs. Star, "take along some of these sandwiches. You're always starving."

Kevin put the sandwiches in his knapsack. "You couldn't starve in these woods if you were gone a week," he said seriously. "Indians lived off the land. We could, too."

"Well, just in case you want something besides berries and wintergreen leaves, the sandwiches will be handy."

Mr. Star walked with the girls and Kevin over to the beginning of the wooded trail. He pointed to a map of the trail. "See? It's a well-marked trail. Take your time and enjoy it. You can't get lost. And when you get back, we'll have trout for dinner—I hope."

Mr. and Mrs. Star took their fishing rods and walked toward the little road leading from the campsite to the lake. "Have fun!" Mrs. Star called and waved.

"I'll lead the way to the trail," announced Kevin.

"Okay, Soaring Beagle," laughed Sally.

"Soaring Eagle," said Kevin, starting into the forest.

"Don't let me out of your sight," said Sally. "Remember, it's my first real hike in the woods."

The trail became narrow. Sally pushed bushes and brambles out of the way. "If this is the start of the trail, what will the rest of it be like?" she groaned.

Kevin was ahead. "I'll be the trailblazer," he said. "I'll go first. Just follow me."

They had only walked a few minutes when Sally suddenly stopped. "Listen!" she whispered. "I hear something. Right in those bushes!"

The three stopped and listened.

"I don't hear anything," said Beth.

"There it is again," whispered Sally. And then they all heard it. Something was moving in the leaves. And then they heard a shrill, angry cry.

·2·

Trouble on the Trail

Sally clutched Beth's sleeve. And then Kevin and Beth laughed, relieved. "It's only a red squirrel," said Kevin.

"Well, it made so much noise I thought it was something being chased by a bear," Sally declared.

"Don't be scared, Princess Trembling Leaf," said Beth. "There isn't anything in this forest that's not afraid of you. Except maybe chipmunks."

"We can feed them after a while," said Kevin, patting his knapsack. "I brought peanuts in the shells."

The three hikers walked along the narrow road. Kevin ran ahead. "Broken Arrow Trail, here we come!" he called.

"I wonder if we'll meet anyone else," said Sally. "Any campers or hikers. Or foxes or snakes."

"We won't run into any people," said Beth. "We always take our camping trip as late in the season as we can. After everyone else. We like to be really private."

"Dad said we are probably the only campers for miles around," said Kevin, running ahead of the girls.

Beth whispered to Sally. "He's in a hurry to get started, but he dawdles when he's on a hike. He likes to stop and look at everything. But I guess that's what hikes are for."

The narrow path curved into the woods.

"It looks as if nobody else has been here in ages," said Sally. She stopped and pulled her sweater away from a bramble.

"We're off in the wild woods!" Kevin announced.

"I wonder why it's called Broken Arrow Trail," said Sally. "It sounds like an Indian name."

"It is," shouted Kevin. He had stopped to

look at a mossy rock. "Indians used to live here a long time ago."

"But why 'Broken'?" asked Sally. "Why not Flying Arrow or something? What good is a broken arrow?"

"You're the Indian expert, Kevin," said Beth. "Why broken arrow?"

"It's not what a broken arrow is, it's what it means," said Kevin. "It means peace. You know, like smoking a peace pipe. When the Indians stopped fighting with another tribe or with outsiders, the chief would break an arrow. Then he'd bury it. That was the Indian way of saying no more fighting."

Kevin leaned over and picked up a leaf.

"And Chief Great Hawk of the O-Wan-Shee tribe was famous for making peace with other tribes. Dad says there's a big rock halfway around on this trail. Great Hawk is supposed to have buried a broken arrow by the rock."

"I hope you know as much about not getting lost as you do about Indians," said Sally.

"We can't get lost if we stay on the trail," said Beth. "Just up the path we'll come to a place where the trail branches in two directions. The trail's like a circle. You can take either path and come back to the place where you started."

The three walked along for another ten minutes. Kevin ran ahead and then lagged behind and then ran ahead again, picking up leaves and stones. He put some of the stones in his knapsack.

"Don't squash our sandwiches," said Sally.

"Here's the fork in the trail," announced Kevin. "Just the way Dad said."

"Which way should we go?" asked Sally.

"I know," suggested Kevin. "You two go left and I'll go right. We can meet halfway, at Chief Great Hawk's rock."

"Won't you be afraid to go alone?" asked Sally. "Aren't you afraid you might get lost?"

"Did you ever hear of anyone named Lightfoot getting lost? Anyway, the two trails aren't far apart. Remember that map on the sign?"

"Lightfoot!" laughed Beth. "What happened to Soaring Eagle?"

"He bit the dust, I guess," said Sally.

"I'll meet you at the Indian rock," said Kevin, starting out on the righthand trail. "Last one there makes breakfast tomorrow."

Beth groaned. "More of your lumpy pancakes."

The two girls started off. In a moment Kevin could no longer see them or hear them laughing as they walked along.

Kevin walked slowly, trying not to miss anything in the woods. He looked up at the tall birch and towering pine trees. He wondered how much he could see if he climbed to the top of a pine. He listened to all the noises of the forest, trying to sort out the different birds and animals.

"Here," he called to a chipmunk. "Here, chippie, here, chippie." He reached into his knapsack for peanuts and tossed some along the trail. A chipmunk scampered over to the peanuts. It picked them up and started stuffing them in its mouth.

In a moment the chipmunk scampered off, its cheeks bulging with the peanuts. The chipmunk wasn't hungry enough—or brave

enough—to eat them there in front of him, Kevin knew.

Again Kevin started up the trail, more quickly this time. But he still watched everything around him and everything he passed. He pretended he really was an Indian scout and tried to move without a sound.

Suddenly Kevin heard a noise coming from up ahead on the trail. Too much noise for a squirrel or chipmunk, he decided. Something was moving through the woods toward the trail just ahead.

He stood and listened. Maybe another hiker, he thought. But in the next moment his heart jumped in sudden shock. Up ahead, something big had stepped onto the trail. It moved slowly and carefully.

Kevin acted fast but quietly. He stepped off the trail into the woods. He stood motionless, holding his breath. He waited. Suddenly he saw what it was. He felt scared from the top of his head down to his toes.

A big black bear was lumbering down the forest trail toward him.

·3·

Loser or Lost?

Beth and Sally were hiking along their side of Broken Arrow trail. Sally was beginning to think Beth was right. There weren't any bears in these woods. She felt a little better.

"If I'm going to be doing all this hiking, I should have a hiking stick," said Sally, glancing around.

"Good idea," said Beth. "I'll find us each one." She peered into the woods. "It really is a jungle in there," she said.

Beth stepped off the trail. The bushes and brambles scratched her. The trees towered above, shutting off most of the light. She quickly found two dead branches of the right size and pushed her way back to the trail.

"If you'd gone one more step into those woods, I couldn't have seen you," said Sally. "It's really thick in there, isn't it?"

Beth nodded. "Your cane, Princess," she said, handing her one of the dead branches.

They walked along the winding trail. "I like this walking stick," Sally said. "I feel braver. I won't worry about snakes along the path." But she did not appear brave as she glanced into the leafy shadows on either side of the trail.

"Mosquitoes, that's what our biggest danger is," said Beth. "And to think I let Kevin go off with the mosquito stuff. It's in his knapsack."

"He's got our sandwiches, too," Sally reminded her.

"And the pickles and the first aid kit and his rocks and sixty-five other things," laughed Beth. "He can't move without his knapsack."

"Listen," whispered Sally suddenly, grabbing Beth's arm. "I hear a snake hissing."

Beth held still. "Silly, that's not a snake. Anyway, there aren't any poisonous snakes up here. Only garter snakes, things like that. And they don't hiss. Or bite," she added, seeing Sally's worried face.

"A snake is a snake," said Sally. "Besides, something's hissing."

Beth listened a moment. "I hear it," she said. "It's a stream. That's not a hiss, it's a gurgle. Let's see if it crosses the trail."

As they walked around the bend in the trail, they saw the stream. A little wooden bridge crossed it.

"Oh, good," said Sally. "A bridge. No swimming, wading, or jumping."

"I'm thirsty," said Beth. "Let's get a drink of water."

"Maybe it'll make us sick," objected Sally. "You should never drink water unless you know it's safe."

"Running water is all right if you skim it from the top," said Beth. "Just don't drink still or stagnant water." She lay on her stomach and reached a hand into the stream. Making a scoop of it, she drank. After Sally had watched a moment, she did the same thing. It was fun.

"Let's pretend we're stranded in the wilderness," suggested Sally. "And we have to catch our own food."

"All right," said Beth. "We could catch fish and cook them."

"And pick blackberries," added Sally.

"And if we get really hungry we can eat grasshoppers and grubs and . . ."

Sally jumped up. "That's enough of *that* game," she said. "Grubs! Grasshoppers!"

Beth laughed. They crossed the wooden bridge over the stream and walked along.

"I'm hungry," said Sally after a while. "Kevin may be hungry, too. He may eat all of the sandwiches before we get there."

"It's farther than I thought," said Beth. "We've been walking over an hour."

As they rounded a bend, Beth saw a figure standing in a clearing. "Hi, Kevin," she shouted. "Sorry we're late."

The figure stood motionless. No one answered. Then Beth saw it wasn't a figure at all. It was the broken trunk of a dead tree that had fooled her. But she did see a big rock just a few steps from the broken tree.

"That has to be Chief Great Hawk's rock," she told Sally.

"But where's Kevin?" asked Sally. "He wanted to get here first. I'm sure of it."

Beth looked around. "This isn't like Kevin," she said after a while. "If he makes a bet, he always makes sure he wins. And he's had plenty of time to get this far."

Suddenly Sally jumped. "Did you hear that?" she whispered.

Beth grinned. "You're always hearing things, Sally. You have good ears for worrying. What is it now?"

"No, really listen," insisted Sally.

Sure enough, in a moment Beth could hear it too, a swishing in the leaves and the sound of something heavy moving through the woods, snapping twigs underfoot.

"It must be Kevin," said Beth, but she frowned. Kevin wouldn't be running through the woods that way. Not unless something was wrong.

"Kevin!" she called.

There was no answer. Whatever had made the sound did not come nearer. The snapping twigs and rustling leaves were softer. The girls listened and heard nothing else.

It could be Kevin trying to play a joke on them, Beth suddenly thought. It didn't seem very funny. "Kevin!" she called again. "We know you're there. Come here!"

There was still no answer. Again Beth wondered if Kevin was in trouble. "I'm going to look around," she announced, walking over to the edge of the woods.

"Don't!" pleaded Sally. "Maybe it isn't Kevin at all. Maybe it's a bear."

"Don't be silly, Sally. I told you there aren't any bears around here." But Beth didn't feel quite so sure of herself as she sounded.

She picked her way around some prickly undergrowth. Someone—or something—must have been here, she decided. They hadn't just imagined the noises. The low-lying forest cover, the little plants and old leaves and twigs, had been trampled down. She tried to see some sort of track but couldn't.

"Kevin!" shouted Beth. "You know what Dad said about going off the trail! You'll get lost!"

There was no answer.

Suddenly Beth's heart started beating fast. That wouldn't have been Kevin. It couldn't have been. He wouldn't do anything dumb like that.

But if it wasn't Kevin, who—or what—was it? She turned quickly and made her way back to the trail.

Sally was crouching behind the Indian rock. "It wasn't Kevin, was it?" she cried.

Beth shook her head.

"But where is he? What's happened?" asked Sally.

Beth frowned and bit her lip. "We'll have to go find him," she decided.

Sally glanced fearfully around her. "What if that was a bear we heard? What if he's in there now? What if he jumps out at us?"

"It wasn't a bear," said Beth positively. But she felt less sure now.

The two girls started walking along the

trail. They stopped to listen. "Kevin!" called Beth.

There was no answer. But maybe around the next bend she'd see him, walking toward them. Maybe.

"Keep your eyes open, Sally," said Beth.

"For the bear?" asked Sally fearfully, peering behind her.

"No, silly. There's no bear following us. Watch for signs of Kevin. He always plays Indian, you know. If he went off the trail for any reason he'd have left a sign for us."

"Maybe he saw a bear and ran back to camp," suggested Sally.

"There is NO bear," repeated Beth slowly. Maybe if she said it out loud a few more times she would really believe it herself.

The girls walked quickly. Beth looked on both sides of the trail for some sign that Kevin had come this far.

"Look!" gasped Sally suddenly, grabbing Beth's arm.

There at the right side of the trail, on a bush, hung Kevin's red cap.

·4·

Clues From Kevin

Beth ran over to the bush. She started to reach for the red cap, then she glanced around quickly.

"He got this far, anyway," she said. "And he hung his cap on this bush—he didn't drop it, and it wasn't caught by a branch."

"Do you think Kevin went back to camp?" asked Sally.

"But why would he leave the trail?" puzzled Beth. She looked at the trees and bushes as if they could answer her. Suddenly she turned to Sally. "I think he was trying to find us." She pointed straight ahead of her, into the woods. "If there were no trees in the way, we'd be able to see the other side of the trail from here, the side we were walking on."

Sally nodded. "Yes, if we had X-ray eyes. So maybe Kevin thought if he walked in a straight line—that way—he'd find us?"

"Yes," agreed Beth. She pointed through the woods. "Kevin went that way to cut us off. He wanted to be sure he wouldn't miss us."

Why had he left the trail? Why was he trying to find them? wondered Beth. He must have wanted to warn them about something. But what?

Sally pointed to the cap. "Then he left that as a clue just in case he missed us."

Beth nodded and walked over to get the cap. She peered into the bushes. Sally was right behind her.

"I don't see anything," said Sally.

"I do," said Beth, pointing. "Look. The bushes are trampled down here. And here are a couple of broken branches. He did go into the woods. He was heading toward the other side of the trail."

"Well, maybe he found the trail. So all we have to do is walk back the way we came. We'll run into him."

Beth shook her head. "Kevin's a good explorer. But he could get lost in woods like these. Once he was in the thick of it, he'd get mixed up."

"You mean he's somewhere in there?" whispered Sally, peering through the tangle of trees and undergrowth.

"I'm afraid so," admitted Beth. "I'll have to go in to look for him."

"Why don't we go back to the campsite and tell your family?" asked Sally. "They could help."

"They're fishing. By the time we'd get back there, and by the time they'd come back with us, it would be late. It would be pretty hard to find Kevin in the dark."

Sally shivered. She pulled her sweater tight around her.

Beth put the red cap on her head. "Something tells me this will take time," she said. "You go on back to the campsite. If Kevin and I aren't there by the time Mom and Dad get back from fishing, you can all come to look for us."

Sally shook her head. "I'm going with you."

Beth turned to her in surprise. "Aren't you afraid?" she asked.

"Of course I'm afraid," said Sally. "I'm scared stiff. But I don't want you to go in there by yourself."

Beth grinned. "I've got to admit I'm glad," she said. "I didn't want to go in there alone. Come on. I know a lot about woods. We won't get lost. We'll find Kevin and we'll find the trail again and we'll be back in time for Dad's fish."

"I hope so," said Sally, crossing her fingers.

The two girls made their way into the woods, Beth leading. A wind had come up. The leaves of the forest whispered and rustled. Sally buttoned her sweater. The girls stopped every few minutes to call Kevin's name.

There was no answer.

"He couldn't hear us call anyway, with all this noise," said Sally. "It's just as if the trees were talking to each other. I wish I understood tree language."

"Look!" shouted Beth. Up ahead, fastened on a low branch of a maple tree, was a strip of red cloth. It was blowing in the breeze. "It's part of Kevin's bandana! He left it for us to see!"

"Well, now we know we're on the right track," said Sally.

"But we don't know how far ahead of us he is. We've got to find him before it starts to get dark. Look for signs. Broken branches. Other pieces of bandana. Anything."

Beth reached into her pocket and took out a scout jackknife. Then she walked over to a nearby tree. She opened the knife and made a mark on the bark.

"What are you doing that for?" asked Sally.

"Well, we don't want to get lost," said Beth. "I should have started doing that in the beginning. It's easy to get mixed up in woods like these." She frowned.

"There's another scrap of bandana," said Sally excitedly. "But which way did he go from here? How can we tell?"

Beth looked around and pointed. "He's

broken some of the lower branches of the trees as a signal," she said. "He knew we could follow him that way. Keep your eyes open. We don't want to lose his trail now."

The girls pushed their way through the woods. Sally stumbled on a dead log and picked herself up, rubbing her knee. "Can't we stop for a few minutes?" she asked.

Beth shook her head. "We've got to keep going. We're on the right track." She called as loud as she could, "Kevin! Kevin!" But there was no answer.

Following the broken branches and strips torn from the bandana, Beth led the way deeper into the forest. She marked the trees as they passed them. If the girls had to go back by the same way, the marks would help them.

"So far, so good," Beth said. But she went only a short distance and stopped to look about. "Now what?" she said under her breath. There were no strips of bandana, no broken branches. Nothing.

"Why did Kevin stop leaving a trail for us?" asked Beth.

"Maybe he ran out of bandana," suggested Sally. "Or maybe he had to run—in a hurry."

Beth stared around her, frowning.

Sally looked up. "It's getting lighter over there," she said, pointing.

Beth looked. Sure enough, it was lighter. Beth thought quickly. Somewhere just ahead there was a place where no trees grew. The trail? She hurried, picking her way carefully through the underbrush. Sally followed her closely. And in a moment they were standing on the edge of a swampy place.

"Quicksand?" whispered Sally, staring.

"No, silly, just a little swamp," said Beth. "But now I know what happened. Kevin was going in a pretty straight line. Then he suddenly saw more light ahead. He decided he'd found the trail. That's what I thought, too, when I saw there was an opening. So he didn't bother to leave any markers behind. He just made his way here—to what he thought would be the trail. But it isn't the trail, it's just a swamp. Then he got mixed up. He didn't know which direction to go."

"Poor Kevin," Sally said. "I know how he felt."

Beth glanced around. "It's easy to lose your bearings in woods like these!"

"And now we'll never find him," said Sally.

"Wait a minute," said Beth slowly. "He'd have followed along the edge of the swamp, sticking to firm ground. But which way?"

"That way," said Sally, sticking her foot into the mushy ground. "It's too soft here. He'd have sunk in. Besides, those brambles would have been too thick—even for an Indian scout."

Beth stooped over, looking hard at the ground where the girls were standing. Then she pointed and said, "He was here."

"I don't see anything," said Sally.

Beth pointed to a bare spot among the weeds. "There was an old log or something here. It's just been moved. Maybe rolled along. See how the plants are knocked down?"

Sally looked around. "Why would Kevin move something heavy?"

Then Beth shouted "There!" and ran toward

the base of a big pine. A rotted log had been rolled over to it.

"He climbed this tree," she said. Both girls tipped their heads back and looked up. The pine was tall and would be easy to climb once the strong branches were reached.

Beth stood on the log and showed Sally how it helped her reach a stout branch. Kevin would have needed that help, too.

"I wonder why he climbed the tree," said Sally. "Maybe to get away from a bear or something."

"No," said Beth. "He wouldn't have had time to move that log." She thought for a moment. "He climbed it because he was lost."

"What good would it do to climb a tree?" asked Sally.

"It might help him get his bearings," said Beth. She stepped onto the log.

"I'm going up there," she announced. "Maybe I'll be able to figure out which way he went."

"Oh, please be careful," said Sally.

"Don't worry," answered Beth. From the log

she was close enough to a low branch to grab it. She wrapped her legs around the trunk, reached up to the branch and pulled herself up. Then she reached up to another branch. Then another.

The branches were closer together now. By staying next to the trunk of the tree, Beth could climb quickly. Very carefully she made her way up the tree. It's lucky I've climbed lots of trees before, she thought.

Soon she was near the top of the tree. She looked straight ahead. She saw nothing but the tops of other trees.

"See anything?" Sally shouted from below.

"Not yet!" answered Beth. She did not look down. Very slowly she turned herself around. She stepped to another branch on the other side of the tree. She peered out. Treetops and sky. She was about to turn when she looked again. A wisp of smoke curling up out of the trees!

Maybe smoke meant a campfire. Kevin must have headed for the smoke, decided Beth. She was sure of that.

·5·

We-no, He-no

"Hey up there!" Sally was shouting and looking up. "See anything?"

"You bet!" yelled Beth. "Smoke!"

"Oh, no!" groaned Sally. "A forest fire!"

"No, silly! A campfire! That's where Kevin must have headed. Smoke means campfire. Campfire means civilization. Anyway, campfire means people." Beth was getting a little dizzy. "I'm coming down!"

"Slowly or all in one bunch?" asked Sally. "Climbing or jumping?"

"Climbing. I forgot my parachute!"

Slowly Beth put her foot on a lower branch. She held onto the trunk and took one last look at the smoke. Then she carefully turned and faced another direction. She wanted to be sure there was nothing else Kevin might have seen.

Slowly she made her way down the tree. In a few minutes she was on the ground again.

"The campfire is thataway," she announced, pointing.

"Whichaway is thataway?" asked Sally. "North, south, east, or west?"

"Well, with no sun I can't tell," admitted Beth. "But it's that way, anyway."

"It's like blindman's buff," said Sally.

"Not quite. When I was up there I figured out how to get to the campfire or at least go in that direction. Between here and there are three huge white birch trees. We can't see them from the ground, but we'll know when we get to them. And Kevin would have gone that way too, I hope. Let's hurry. Now we know which way he was heading. And now we know he knew he was lost."

"We know he knows," said Sally. "That's my new name: We-no he-no."

"All right, We-no he-no, this is our plan. Kevin knew he was lost when he climbed the tree. Getting to the swamp had thrown him off the track. Before that, he had thought he was on a straight line to us. But he lost his bearings. So he climbed up to get a look around. And all he could see were tops of trees. And the smoke. So he must have decided to follow the smoke."

Sally nodded. "It's like a mystery. But how does he know we're following him?"

Beth shrugged. "Because he knows me," she said after a minute. "He knows I'd look for him."

"He-no, you-no. We-no, me-no," said Sally, saluting. "Going off the trail is no-no, right?"

Beth nodded. "Yes-yes, it's no-no, and he knew it. So he must have done it for a very important reason."

Sally's face clouded over. "And the important reason may be an important bear. An important bear could be an important reason for Kevin finding us. And us finding Kevin. And the bear finding us. And—"

"Come on, silly," said Beth, starting to walk again. Sally might think she was joking with that kind of talk, but she could scare them both. "Look for other pieces of his bandana or marks on a tree. Or broken branches. Anything." Beth had to keep Sally busy.

"How to get eaten by a bear in one easy lesson," said Sally. But she followed Beth and kept her eyes open for any sign of Kevin.

"How do you know where you're going?" she asked Beth. "Maybe we're going in circles." She stopped to free her sweater from a bush.

"I don't think so," said Beth. "If I'm right, we're heading for the three white birches."

"All trees look alike to me," said Sally.

"Well, probably all people look alike to trees," answered Beth. "You and I may be dressed alike, but people can tell us apart."

Sally laughed. "Well, my name's Sally and your name's Beth, for one thing."

"And this is white pine and that over there is tamarack," said Beth.

"There are so many kinds," sighed Sally.

"And so many kinds of people," answered Beth.

"I've never seen so many trees in my life.

And I bet these trees have never seen so many people. I bet we're the first people here since Indians long ago."

"Except Kevin," said Beth, pointing. Sure enough, on the branch of a tree just ahead was another little piece of Kevin's red bandana.

"What will he do when he runs out of bandana?" asked Sally.

"He'll think of something," Beth assured her. "He's hanging onto his clothes because of the brambles."

"And the mosquitoes," groaned Sally, scratching her arm.

They both heard it at the same time. A rushing of water.

"The stream!" shouted Beth.

"The same one we crossed?" asked Sally.

"It must be." Beth thought quickly. The patch of woods that was surrounded by the Broken Arrow Trail was a very big patch indeed. Bigger than she first thought. And in spite of everything she had done, Beth was afraid she was really lost, too.

Soon the woods would be dark. The trees

were so tall they blocked out the light as the sun went down.

The stream sounded as if it were only a few yards ahead. If they followed it, they would find the trail. Not Kevin, but the trail.

She decided to follow the sound of the water. It wouldn't do Kevin any good if she and Sally got themselves lost, too. And if they found the stream again, she knew they could find the trail. But they had to find Kevin. She sighed. First the stream. Then Kevin. Then back to the stream, and then back to the trail. She'd have to be very careful to leave markers behind so they could find their way back to the stream after they found Kevin. *If* they found Kevin.

In a few minutes the girls came upon the rushing stream. It was wider here than it was when they had crossed it before. "Wider and deeper," said Sally, peering down at it. "And if we follow it, we'll find the trail again, right?"

"Yes," said Beth thoughtfully. "We'll find the trail. But Kevin didn't know that. He was still trying to follow the smoke. So he would have crossed the stream. I'm sure of it."

"But wouldn't he have known that the stream would have had to cross the trail?" asked Sally.

"Sometimes a stream goes underground and you lose it. It wasn't marked on the map at the start of the trail. He would follow the smoke," said Beth. "Let's try to find where he crossed the stream."

"It's too wide to jump across," said Sally firmly. "No bridge either."

Beth crouched down at the side of the stream. She looked up and down. Suddenly she jumped up. "Kevin must have waded. Or made himself a bridge."

"A bridge of what?" asked Sally.

"A log. A dead tree. Rocks for stepping stones. There's got to be some clue. Let's follow the bank and see."

They began making their way through the thick brush that grew so well next to the water.

"Look!" said Sally.

Beth peered down at the bank of the stream. There was a footprint.

·6·

Save Our Skin!

There in the wet sand next to the stream was the footprint of a shoe. "It's Kevin's!" shouted Beth.

"Kevin's? How do you know for sure? Maybe it's a bear track!" teased Sally to keep from feeling scared.

"Kevin's shoe has a broken cleat on it. And you can see where the heel of this print is broken. See? And bears don't wear shoes."

"Okay, so it's Kevin's. Now what?" asked Sally.

"Look!" Beth pointed to a dead tree in the water. "He must have pushed that log around and crawled across it. Let's try it!"

The girls struggled with the tree. They held one end. The tree bobbed in the water. Then

finally it snagged on a big rock near the other side.

"I'll go first," announced Beth. "You hold onto me. We'll go very slowly."

Carefully the girls climbed onto the slippery log and started crawling.

"What if we fall off?" asked Sally nervously.

"It's not that deep. The worst you'll get is wet."

"Then I'll just close my eyes and hang on tight."

Beth moved slowly, aware of the tug from behind. In a minute Beth said, "Open your eyes, silly!"

Sally opened her eyes. Then she climbed carefully off the log. She sat down next to a tree. "I guess you're more used to this than I am. I'm tired. And I'm starving. And I'm scared. And it's getting dark. But at least I'm not alone." She added, "If I were all alone, I'd just sit here crying."

"That would be very helpful," laughed Beth.

Sally looked at the arm of her sweater. "I'm

unraveling," she said. "One snag too many, I guess. And that's just the way I'm beginning to feel. All unraveled." She sighed and looked around. "Where did Kevin go from here?" she asked. "He must have left us a clue."

Beth frowned. "I don't see any red bandana. I don't see any broken branches."

Sally got to her feet. She had to be sensible, she told herself. "Maybe Kevin didn't cross the stream just where we did," she said. "Maybe we should walk along the edge for a way. Do you think so?"

"Okay," agreed Beth. "Let's look for some kind of signal he left for us to find."

They picked their way along the stream, first one way, then another, looking for some sign that Kevin had been there.

Suddenly Beth started to laugh. Sally looked over. Beth pointed. "Did you ever see a tree with a bandage?" she asked. "I guess he ran out of bandana and started on his first aid kit!"

Sure enough, on a low branch of a tree next to the stream a white gauze bandage was fluttering gently in the breeze.

"And here on the next tree is a broken branch," announced Sally. "So we know what direction he was heading, anyway. Let's go." She was getting more used to this tracking business.

"Wait a minute," said Beth thoughtfully. "We came pretty close to getting lost ourselves. It's going to be getting dark. We've got to find a foolproof way to get back here to the stream—once we find Kevin," she said. "Otherwise there will be three people lost instead of just one."

"How about the way you were marking the trees with your pocketknife?" asked Sally.

"That won't do us much good in the dark," answered Beth. "It's got to be something we can *feel*. If only we had a ball of twine. We could string it along as we went."

Sally scratched her arm. "I've got a big ball of yarn," she said, "if that will help us."

Beth glanced over at her. "Where?" she asked. "What do you mean?"

"Well, it's a sweater now, but it *was* a big

ball of yarn, about a couple thousand knits and purls ago. We could use that."

"Perfect!" grinned Beth.

"Let's hurry," said Sally. "If it gets too dark we won't be able to see any strips of gauze. Or any Kevin, either."

"Once we find him we can get back to the stream by following the yarn," said Beth. "It will be the fastest way back to the trail." Sally's idea was a good one.

Sally started quickly to unravel a sleeve of her sweater.

Beth tied one end of the yarn to the trunk of a tree. Then, following the white fluttering pieces of gauze, they started picking their way through the forest, unraveling the sweater as they went. Beth wrapped the yarn around the trunk of a little tree, then walked farther along. She wrapped the yarn around another tree, then another, leading into the forest.

They followed the strips of white gauze.

"Why didn't he make us a trail of peanuts to follow?" asked Sally. "We could have eaten them."

"The chipmunks and squirrels would have beaten us to them," said Beth.

"Chipmunks," said Sally. "The ones you see are probably just babies. Deep in the woods maybe they grow to be as big as bears."

"Silly," answered Beth.

Suddenly they heard something. They stopped in their tracks.

Beth held her breath. There *was* something. A sound that came over the sound of the whispering trees. It seemed almost as if it came from the ground itself.

"Maybe it's a troll," whispered Sally.

"Listen," said Beth.

"Let's put our ears to the ground," suggested Sally.

"Don't be silly," said Beth, but in an instant she had followed Sally's lead and was kneeling with her ear to the ground.

She could hear a thumping. It was a regular beat. What was it?

"Indian drums?" suggested Sally. "War dance, maybe," she added, still trying to keep her fear away by joking.

"Shhh," whispered Beth, trying to listen.

In a few moments a pattern emerged. Three short thumps, three long thumps, three short thumps.

"It's an SOS!" shouted Beth. "It's Kevin, and he's thumping something to let us know where he is."

"How do you know?" asked Sally, still bending over with her ear to the ground.

"SOS. Three shorts, three longs, three shorts," explained Beth excitedly.

"S-O-S," repeated Sally, standing up. "Save our skin." She dusted herself off. "Now what? We know he's signaling to us, but where is the sound coming from?"

Beth stood and listened. She frowned. "It's hard to tell. Sounds can fool you in the woods," she said finally. "But at least we know he's somewhere safe."

"Safe? How do you know a big bear isn't walking up to him right now?" asked Sally.

"He wouldn't have time to send messages," Beth answered sensibly. She listened another moment. "It's coming from this way, I think," she announced, pointing. "Let's try it."

The two started off toward the sound of the thumping. It seemed to grow louder.

Beth started to shout. "Kevin! Hallloooooo, Kevin!"

"He'll never hear you over that drum," said Sally.

"Shhh—" said Beth.

They listened. They kept calling, "Kevin! Kevin!" and then Beth heard his voice: "Ho yo, ho yo. Over here!"

"Stay there!" shouted Beth, her voice straining.

They called back and forth.

"Hotter, colder," Sally kept saying out loud as they zigzagged trying to locate the sound. Then Beth saw Kevin.

He was sitting next to a hollow log, hitting it with a thick broken branch.

"Oh, Kevin!" said Beth. She was smiling, but she had a lump in her throat.

·7·

Home Safe?

"There's a bear—" Kevin started to say.

Sally jumped and screamed, "Where?"

"I saw it on the trail! It was right ahead of me. I had to warn you. I thought it might follow the trail and—find you." Kevin swallowed.

"So you left the trail and cut across the forest to try to find us?" said Beth.

"Even knowing you might run into the bear?" said Sally, wonderingly. "And get lost?"

Kevin nodded.

"But what about the bear? Where is he now?" asked Sally.

Kevin jumped up. "Who knows? I don't. What I do know is that he's more afraid of us than we are of him. All we have to do is find our way back to camp. And let someone know there's a bear out here."

"What makes you think he's more afraid than I am?" asked Sally. "I'm so scared I can't move."

"When you're too scared to talk, then you'll know you're really scared," Kevin laughed.

"Maybe if I have one of those sandwiches I'll feel better," groaned Sally. The two girls ate and talked.

"We can find our way back to the trail," Beth told Kevin. "We unraveled Sally's sweater."

"You're a better scout than I was," sighed Kevin. "I got lost there at the swamp. Then I tried to follow some smoke. And then I thought I'd better sit still and wait until you found me."

"Well, we'd have been lost, too," Beth assured him. "But we found the stream."

"I found the stream, too," said Kevin. "But I couldn't be sure it would cross the trail."

"We knew it did," explained Sally. "We crossed it on our way to the Indian rock. If we follow the stream we can find the trail again."

Beth grinned at Sally. "I welcome you to the Indian Tribe of Star."

Sally looked around the trees. "There *was* a bear. There was a bear all along," she whispered. "I was right after all. And now he's going to come after us, I know it. I just know it."

"Don't be silly, Sally," said Beth, but she glanced around nervously.

"Bears don't chase people," said Kevin. "They wouldn't even like the taste of you."

"Don't say that," shuddered Sally.

Beth motioned to the yarn. "If the bear comes, we can tie him up, Sally. So don't worry. Come on, let's get back to the stream."

The three took a last look around the clearing. Then they turned to follow the trail of yarn.

"I'll go first," said Beth.

"I'll bring up the rear," offered Kevin.

"Let's go," said Beth. "We can still make it back to the stream and then to the trail and then to the campsite before it gets too dark."

The three hikers followed the yarn.

"Hey, Kevin! Keep moving! You've got to

keep up with us!" called Beth from time to time.

Suddenly Beth said happily, "I hear it! We're near the stream!" She ran ahead.

Beth looked back at Sally and grinned. "Home safe!" she started to say.

But Sally was clutching a tree, eyes wide open, staring at the stream.

Beth looked toward the stream through the trees. And then she saw it. Standing at the shore, drinking from the water, was a big black bear.

"Kevin!" whispered Beth sharply. She kept her eyes on the huge animal. "Stay put!"

Kevin took one silent step behind a tree and froze, holding his breath.

Beth turned her head very slowly toward Sally. "He hasn't heard us," she said in a tiny whisper. "Don't move. He doesn't know we're here."

Sally's eyes were still wide and her mouth was open. Beth knew that Kevin would stay still and quiet. And she hoped the bear would do no harm unless it was frightened or injured.

But Sally was scared enough to do something foolish.

All three stared at the bear. They didn't move.

Suddenly the bear lifted his mouth out of the water and put his nose in the air. The bear smelled something different. He bobbed his head in the air, trying to pick up the smell.

And then Sally snapped out of her trance. She gasped and stepped backward in fright. Right behind her was a log. She tripped on it, fell backward, and screamed.

The bear jerked around. He stood up on his hind legs. The three saw in horror how huge he was. He dropped quickly to all four feet and began to run toward the hikers.

Oh no! thought Beth. He's going for Kevin!

The bear was at a full lumbering run. He shot past Beth and Sally and headed straight for Kevin.

Kevin stood frozen, facing the charging bear. The bear seemed to grow larger and larger every second. When the bear was almost upon him, Kevin closed his eyes. Sally screamed again. The bear's fur swished against Kevin's arm as it ran by. Still Kevin didn't move a muscle.

When the crashing of twigs and branches grew quieter and the bear was far off, Kevin quietly slumped down. He leaned against the tree.

Sally and Beth ran over to him. Both girls had tears in their eyes. "Are you okay, Kevin?" asked Beth.

"I'm okay," said Kevin, as the three put their arms around each other. "At least I think I am. Anyway, I think I'm alive."

"Not me," said Sally. "I'll never be the same."

The three sat by the tree, waiting for their hearts to stop racing.

"My legs turned to Jello," said Kevin sheepishly.

"If I hadn't screamed and fallen, the bear wouldn't have bothered us," said Sally after a while.

"You were very brave," Beth assured her.

"It's funny that a bear was around here. He

must have been lost," said Kevin, puzzled.

"Like us," said Sally.

"We're not lost now," said Beth, jumping to her feet. "We'll just follow the stream to the trail. Come on!"

"I don't know whether my legs will work," said Kevin.

The three walked over to the stream and started moving along its edge, through the thick brush.

"Let's hurry," urged Sally.

"Don't worry," said Kevin. "It's not as dark as it looks."

"What does that mean?" asked Sally. "What other way can you tell how dark it is, except by how it looks?"

"How it feels," laughed Kevin. "What I meant was that it's darker here in the woods than it will be on the trail."

Beth was the first to see it. "The trail!" she breathed.

"Home safe," said Kevin.

"Not yet," Sally reminded him.

They started down the trail.

Suddenly they heard a crunching on the path ahead of them. They stopped, clutching each other. Someone was coming closer. Someone or something. It couldn't be the bear—or could it?

"Let's hide," whispered Kevin. They ran quickly to the side of the trail and stumbled into the bushes. They crouched there, afraid to breathe. Their hearts pounded.

And then they heard someone humming. Sally gasped in relief. "Bears don't hum!"

In a moment a tall man in ranger uniform rounded the curve. The three stepped out from the bushes and onto the trail.

They all started to talk at once. When the ranger heard the word "bear," he frowned. "We were afraid of that," he said. "They're building a big sawmill a little farther north. We thought maybe a couple of the old bears would be pushed out of their territory. We were right. Was this one a black middle-sized bear?"

"No," answered Sally. "It was a *huge* bear, a giant bear, as big as a mountain."

Kevin interrupted. "As bears go, I guess it was a middle-sized one," he said. "With one short ear."

The ranger smiled. "That's old Banjo. He's pretty far from his home base. He might have been a little nervous, but he wouldn't cause any harm unless he was very frightened. He almost never sees any humans, you know."

"He saw us," Sally said.

"I'll walk back to camp with you," the ranger suggested. "Then I'll round up a couple of guys and we'll get old Banjo back to where he belongs. Sorry he gave you a scare."

"Oh, we weren't scared at all," said Kevin. "Maybe he was, but we weren't."

"Not very scared, anyway," said Beth.

"I was," said Sally. "Scared silly."

"You were really the bravest of all, then," Beth told her. "Because you came along and you did it all, scared or not.

"And that's really being brave, Princess Trembling Leaf," added Kevin, winking at her.